SMART SURVIVORS

Twelve of the Earth's Most Remarkable Living Things

By Sneed B. Collard III

NorthWord PRESS

Minnetonka, Minnesota

For Rich Moser,
a fellow survivor in good times and bad.

Edited by Greg Linder
Designed by Patricia Bickner Linder

COWLES
Creative Publishing, Inc.

NorthWord Press
5900 Green Oak Drive
Minnetonka, MN 55343
1-800-328-3895

Library of Congress Cataloging-in-Publication Data

Collard, Sneed B.
    Smart Survivors / by Sneed Collard.
        p.   cm.
    Summary: Introduces plants and animals that do "smart" things to assure their survival.
Includes nudibranches, kangaroo rats, and strangler figs.
        ISBN 1-55971-643-6
    1. Competition (Biology)—Juvenile literature. [1. Animals—Miscellanea. 2. Plants—
Miscellanea.]   I. Title.
QH546.3.C65   1994
574.5'247—dc20   93–19650
                                                                      CIP
                                                                      AC

Printed in Singapore

TABLE OF CONTENTS

About Survivors

We've all got problems. We're behind in our homework. Our hair is too long or too short. Our sisters or brothers keep borrowing our clothes. Some days we have more problems than we know what to do with! But we have other problems that we usually don't even think about.

Each day we need enough water to drink and enough food to eat. We need to stay warm and breathe enough oxygen. We need a place to live, and we need to communicate with the people around us. If we did not solve each of these problems, we would soon perish.

In order to survive, animals and plants face many of the same problems. Different organisms solve these problems in an astounding variety of ways. Each method works for that species, but some plants and animals survive in ways that seem *especially* amazing or "smart."

In this book you'll meet some of the smartest survivors on our planet. You'll learn how they defend themselves, how they get enough food and water, and how they solve other problems. As you read, think about the problems each survivor faces, and think about how other animals and plants solve the same problems. You might be surprised to realize that each and every living thing—including you and me—is a smart survivor in its own special way.

DASHING DEFENDERS
Nudibranchs

GARY MILBURN/TOM STACK AND ASSOCIAT

When we think about survival, one of the first things likely to pop into our heads is finding enough food. But for most plants and animals, it's just as important to avoid *becoming* food. Some animals use claws or scales to avoid being eaten. Others hide from their enemies. Among the all-time self-defense champions, though, is a group of sea slugs called nudibranchs (NOOD-I-BRANKS).

Nudibranchs are closely related to snails and land slugs. Like land slugs, nudibranchs have no shells to protect them. Being shell-less could make nudibranchs easy targets for predators. But nudibranchs aren't as defenseless as they seem. Many species blend in with their surroundings, so predators have a hard time seeing them. Other nudibranchs display dazzling shades of orange, violet, red, and yellow as a warning to predators: "If you eat me, you'll be sorry!"

About 2,500 species of nudibranchs live in the world's oceans. Most are found in the warm waters of the tropics, but nudibranchs live in colder waters, too. Some nudibranchs are so small they fit between grains of sand. Others grow to over 12 inches. Most are about an inch long.

Where nudibranchs live

Predators pay attention to a nudibranch's colorful warning for good reasons. The skin of many nudibranchs is filled with acids and other chemicals that make the sea slugs taste bad. Other nudibranchs are armed with stinging cells called **nematocysts** (NEE-MAT-O-SISTS). Amazingly, the nudibranchs have to steal their stinging cells from other creatures.

Nudibranchs steal stingers from sea anemones, corals, and other animals they eat that are loaded with nematocysts. The stingers are like little poison darts that "fire" when they're touched by unwelcome visitors. Some kinds of nudibranchs, though, can swallow nematocysts without triggering them. Instead, the nudibranchs store the stinging cells in the feathery projections on their backs. When a predator tries to touch or bite one of these nudibranchs—OUCH!—the stingers fire, and the showy sea slugs go their own way.

WATER WIZARDS
Kangaroo Rats

A water wheel won't turn unless water is flowing through it. Life on the earth is the same way. Without water, all living things would grind to a halt. People and other mammals are especially dependent on water. To survive, an adult human must take in about two and a half quarts of water each day. Water is so important that most mammals can't survive in a dry desert. But kangaroo rats are able to do just that.

WENDY SHATTIL/BOB ROZINSKI/TOM STACK AND ASSOCIATES

Most mammals need a lot of water because they *lose* a lot of water. Mammals lose a lot of water simply by breathing. Before air enters a mammal's lungs, it must be warmed and moistened by special tissues in the animal's nose called **mucous membranes**. When a mammal breathes out again, it often loses all the water in that warm, moist air.

Kangaroo rats, though, have a "nose for water." When a kangaroo rat breathes out, the water in its breath collects like dew inside the rat's nostrils. In this way, the rat recycles the water, using it again and again.

Kangaroo rats are small rodents that inhabit open, arid places such as the Great Plains and the deserts of the Southwest. They live from southern Canada to Mexico. There are about 24 species of these hopping rodents and, not including their handsome tails, they're four to six-and-a-half inches long. They're named for their kangaroo-style hop, but don't be fooled: Kangaroo rats are not kangaroo kin.

Where kangaroo rats live

To save water, kangaroo rats also look beyond the ends of their noses. The animals have no sweat glands, so they don't lose water by perspiring through their skin. They also have special kidneys that use just one-fifth the amount of water human kidneys need to get rid of bodily wastes. And kangaroo rats spend their days in underground burrows, where they stay cool and moist even in scorching weather.

How do these desert rats get water in the first place? The answer is surprising: They eat seeds. The seeds look dry, but to the kangaroo rat they are instant water holes. As it eats, a kangaroo rat absorbs water from the seeds. Even more water is released when the seeds are broken down by the kangaroo rat's body. "Squeezing" seeds allows kangaroo rats to live in the driest deserts without drinking a drop.

LOVERS OF LIGHT
Strangler Figs

JOH

Plants are boring, right? Wrong! Plants—like animals—are often locked in deadly contests to get enough energy, nutrients, space, and water. In rain forests, so many plants and trees grow so close together that sunlight is in short supply. One group of plants called **epiphytes** (EP-I-FITES) gets around this problem by living in the tops of trees and in other plants. Many epiphytes do not harm the plants they live in, but strangler figs will kill for a little sunlight.

KEVIN SCHAFER/MARTHA HILL/TOM STACK AND ASSOCIATES

Most trees start life in the ground but not strangler figs. Their seeds spr in the tops of other trees, where they dropped by fig-eating birds, bats, and other animals. In the top of the tree, strangler fig seed receives plenty of sunlight and starts growing. New branches and leaves climb toward the sky, while roots snake down the trunl the fig's "host tree." The strangler's r hold the young fig tree in place, and when the roots reach the ground, the start absorbing nutrients and water th the fig needs to grow.

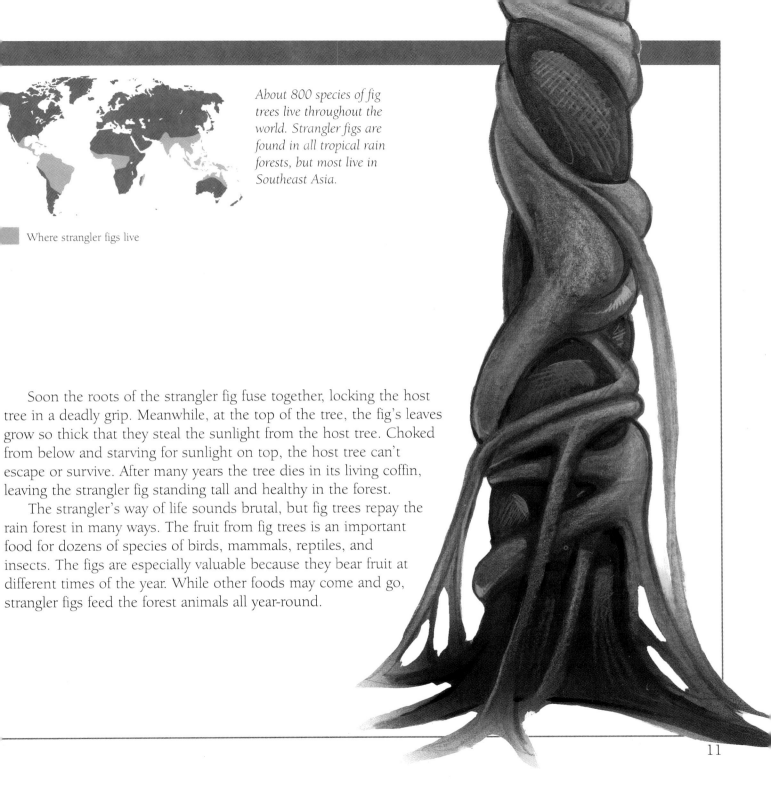

About 800 species of fig trees live throughout the world. Strangler figs are found in all tropical rain forests, but most live in Southeast Asia.

Where strangler figs live

Soon the roots of the strangler fig fuse together, locking the host tree in a deadly grip. Meanwhile, at the top of the tree, the fig's leaves grow so thick that they steal the sunlight from the host tree. Choked from below and starving for sunlight on top, the host tree can't escape or survive. After many years the tree dies in its living coffin, leaving the strangler fig standing tall and healthy in the forest.

The strangler's way of life sounds brutal, but fig trees repay the rain forest in many ways. The fruit from fig trees is an important food for dozens of species of birds, mammals, reptiles, and insects. The figs are especially valuable because they bear fruit at different times of the year. While other foods may come and go, strangler figs feed the forest animals all year-round.

TWILIGHT TALKERS
Fireflies

Communication is important to almost every animal. People communicate by talking, by writing, and even by stomping up and down. Other animals communicate in astonishing ways, but one way seems almost magical—the firefly's light.

ROBERT AND LINDA MITCHELL

Plants, animals, and other organisms that make their own light are called **bioluminescent** (BI-O-LOOM-I-NEH-SENT). Hundreds of organisms, from fungi and worms to fish and squid, are bioluminescent. Some organisms use light to attract prey. Others use it to blend in with their surroundings. However, the firefly is one of the few animals that uses light to "talk" to its own kind.

Fireflies aren't really flies. They're beetles. Fireflies live all over the world, including North America, but most live in the tropics. All together, there are about 2,000 species.

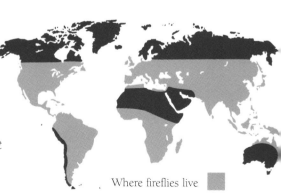

Where fireflies live

12

A firefly's light is produced by chemical reactions that take place inside the "light organ" on its abdomen. Fireflies use light mostly to attract mates, but different fireflies talk in different ways. In North America, the males of several species fly around while the females sit on the ground or on leaves. When a male firefly flashes, the female flashes back, which helps the male find her. If the female flashes too soon or waits too long, the male instinctively knows he is talking to the wrong species, so he stays away.

Flashes can be deceptive, though. The female of one kind of firefly sometimes imitates other firefly species. After she has mated with a male of her own species, she flashes at males of *other* species. The males land near her so they can mate. Instead of mating with these males, the female firefly eats them!

The most spectacular fireflies of all are the synchronous (SING-KRO-NUS) fireflies of Southeast Asia. Just after sunset, thousands of male synchronous fireflies start to flash, lighting up entire riverbanks in flashes of dazzling yellow. Scientists aren't sure why the fireflies flash at the same time, but that doesn't keep us from appreciating one of nature's most "illuminating" experiences.

ROBERT AND LINDA MITCHELL

ENERGY EXPERTS

Deep-Sea Vent Organisms

We are often taught that the energy for all life forms comes from the sun. The sun supplies energy so plants can grow. In turn, animals eat the plants—or they eat other animals that eat plants. But in 1977, a discovery at the bottom of the ocean changed our ideas about life on Earth. Scientists discovered a whole group of life forms that survive without any energy from the sun. These life forms are called deep-sea vent organisms.

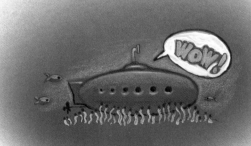

Deep-sea vents are streams of hot water that bubble up from the ocean floor. They exist where large pieces of the earth's crust called **tectonic plates** are sliding together or spreading apart. Scientists found the deep-sea vents while they were exploring the ocean in submarines. When they discovered the vents, they were stunned. Hundreds of animals surrounded the vents—animals no one had ever seen before.

No one knew how these animals managed to survive, but it didn't take long to solve the riddle. The answer lay in a group of tiny organisms called bacteria. Bacteria live almost everywhere. Most eat other things or use the sun's energy to make their own food. But the deep-sea vent bacteria get energy by splitting chemicals called **sulfides**, which are found in the hot water that pours out of the vents. Later, the bacteria use this energy to make food for themselves.

DUDLEY FOSTER, WOODS HOLE OCEANOGRAPHIC INSTITUTION

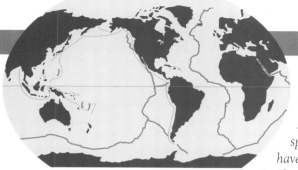

Deep-sea vents are found in areas where tectonic plates are sliding together or spreading apart. Vents have been discovered in the Pacific, Atlantic, and Indian oceans. Most deep-sea vents are no more than a few yards across, but in 1993, scientists discovered a vent field that covers 50 acres.

Anemones, mussels, shrimp, and limpets all feast on deep-sea bacteria. However, the most interesting vent animals are huge tubeworms called "vestimentiferans" (VEST-I-MEN-TI-FER-ENZ). These tubeworms grow over five feet high and form "worm gardens" around the deep-sea vents. The tubeworms have sulfide-splitting bacteria living inside their bodies. Both the worms and the bacteria benefit from this arrangement. The bacteria make food for the worms, while the worms give the bacteria a place to live.

HEAT HOGGERS
Polar Bears

Staying warm is a must for mammals. People stay warm by bundling up in coats and sweaters, or by staying indoors on cold days. But polar bears live outside in temperatures that reach 60 degrees below zero. How do they do it?

The first polar bears "hit the ice" between 100,000 and 200,000 years ago. Since then, the bears have evolved remarkable ways to stay warm in their freezing world. First of all, they have a thick layer of fat called blubber beneath their skin. Blubber insulates them from cold water, snow, and ice.

Polar bears live in one of Earth's harshest environments—the arctic. There, the bears prefer to live along the edges of the large ice sheets that cover the Arctic Ocean for much of the year. Polar bears also roam across the frozen arctic regions of Canada, Alaska, Greenland, the former Soviet Union, and other northern countries.

 Where polar bears live

Polar bears eat mostly fat and meat—high-energy food that is converted into heat by the bears' bodies. To save energy, the bears sleep a lot, sometimes dozing off in the middle of a snow drift.

The most impressive thing that keeps a polar bear warm is its fur. A bear's fur is not really white—it's transparent. Each hair is like a tiny glass fiber that carries light from the sun to the bear. Beneath its "glass coat," the polar bear has black skin that absorbs heat very efficiently, keeping the animal warm.

A polar bear's fur converts 95 percent of the energy from light into heat—that's more than twice as efficient as any solar energy collector that people have invented. Scientists are studying polar bear fur so we can invent better ways to capture the sun's rays. Just by staying warm, polar bears may help us meet our future energy needs.

CLEVER CONSTRUCTORS
Weaver Ants

Everyone needs a place to live—even an ant. But finding a home is not always easy. Space on the ground may already be occupied. Cracks and crevices on plants and rocks may be in short supply. However, one group of ants weaves its way around this problem—the weaver ants.

Weaver ants build their own homes by using their body silk to "weave" tree leaves together. First, worker ants scout around in a tree, looking for places that would make good nest sites. When one worker manages to pull a leaf edge back on itself or pull two leaves together, other worker ants rush to help out.

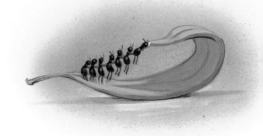

ROBERT AND LINDA MITCHELL

Several kinds of weaver ants build their own homes. The finest "ant architects"—those that build the most sophisticated shelters—live in the forested parts of tropical Africa, and from India to Australia and the Solomon Islands.

■ Where weaver ants live

Weaver ants live in colonies of up to half a million ants. A colony may inhabit more than 150 nests spread across several trees, but the ants use a nest only while its leaves are fresh. As soon as the leaves turn brown, they build a new nest. By building their own houses, weaver ants can survive in much larger numbers than insects that have to "find" houses.

By working together, ants pull the leaves into a shape that looks like a tent. Sometimes long chains of worker ants hold onto each other and pull leaves together.

When the leaves are in the right place, another group of worker ants carries weaver ant larvae out from nearby nests. The larvae make a silk or "glue" that dries quickly. By moving the larvae from place to place, the worker ants cement the leaves into a cozy nest about the size of a small coconut.

Weaver ants also protect the trees they live in by eating beetles and other animals that may damage trees. For over 1,700 years, Chinese people have used weaver ants to protect fruit trees from insect pests. Using ants to control pests is the earliest known example of **biological pest control** in human history.

NUTRIENT NABBERS
Cleaner Wrasses

People use weaver ants and other animals to control pests, but pest control in wild places often happens naturally. Many fish and other animals control pests simply by eating them. Among the flashiest of these nutrient nabbers are the "cleaner" wrasses.

MIKE SEVERNS/TOM STACK AND ASSOCIATES

Cleaner wrasses survive by picking dead tissue and **parasites** off of other fish. The parasites include fungi, bacteria, and small, shrimplike animals called **crustaceans** (KRUS-TAY-SHUNS). Parasites live on the skin, fins, and gills of all fish, and they can harm a fish by sucking its blood or eating its tissues.

To nab these parasites, cleaner wrasses set up "cleaning stations," usually next to a rock or a piece of coral. A cleaning station is like a car wash for fish. "Customers" are attracted by the wrasses' bright colors, and by a special swimming dance that the wrasses perform.

Wrasses live all over the world. One kind of wrasse called the giant wrasse grows over seven feet long, but most cleaner wrasses are shorter than a pencil. Cleaner wrasses are most often found in tropical waters.

Where cleaner wrasses live

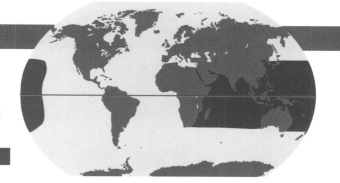

Fish that want to be cleaned hover next to the cleaning station, spreading out their fins and opening their mouths and gills. This kind of "posing" helps the wrasses find parasites and dead tissue.

Working alone or in pairs, cleaner wrasses swim all around their customer fish, picking parasites off with their sharp, tweezer-like teeth. The customers are usually much bigger than the wrasses. They could easily swallow the cleaners, but instead they wait patiently. Many fish even let the wrasses swim safely inside their gills and mouths.

Hundreds of fish species stay healthier by visiting cleaning stations. The cleaning service helps the wrasses, too. They could find food almost anywhere, but cleaning stations make life easier. For them, it's like having a "parasite pizza" delivered to their home every day of the week.

MARVELOUS MOVERS
Snakes

Kangaroos hop, birds fly, and people walk. Most of Earth's animals are on the move. Few methods of motion are more mysterious, spectacular, and startling than the sly slithering of snakes.

To get an idea of what it's like to be a snake, try sliding across a carpet on your belly, without using your arms or legs. For humans it's almost impossible, but for snakes it's a snap.

Snakes actually move in several ways. **Sidewinding** is the showiest. Sidewinding is used by snakes that move across sand or other shifting surfaces. A sidewinder keeps parts of its body pressed against the sand, while throwing or pulling the rest of its body forward. The name "sidewinding" comes from the fact that the snake's body is sideways to the direction that the snake is traveling.

Another popular snake movement is called **serpentine locomotion** (SUR-PEN-TEEN LO-KUH-MO-SHUN) because so many snakes, or "serpents," use it. In serpentine locomotion, a snake uses the sides of its body to push off of several different objects at once. These objects can be rocks, twigs, or even blades of grass. The snake's constant pushing allows it to move forward smoothly without using a lot of energy.

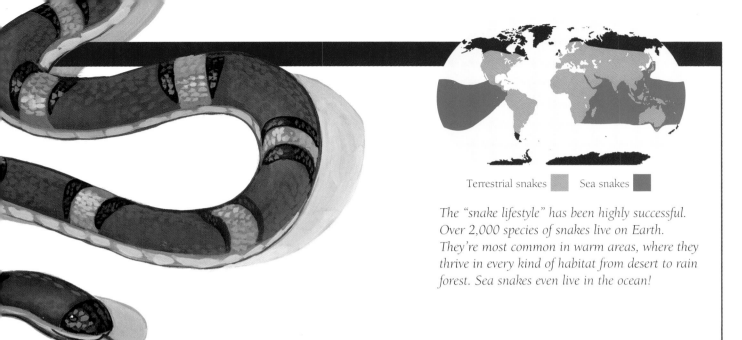

Terrestrial snakes ☐   Sea snakes ■

The "snake lifestyle" has been highly successful. Over 2,000 species of snakes live on Earth. They're most common in warm areas, where they thrive in every kind of habitat from desert to rain forest. Sea snakes even live in the ocean!

A third snake motion is **rectilinear** (REK-TI-LIN-E-AR) **movement**, which lets snakes creep straight ahead without bending. A snake accomplishes this by gripping the ground with its "scutes" or belly scales, then sliding its body forward inside of its skin. Once the body has moved forward, the skin "lets go" of the ground and catches up.

Snakes also jump, swim, ripple, and glide through the air. Scientists have discovered that when snakes move, they use about the same amount of energy a lizard uses to walk. But living without legs gives snakes an advantage—it lets them slip through holes and into tight places, where they can find food and rest up for another day of slithering.

C. ALLAN MORGAN

23

REMARKABLE REPRODUCERS
Bucket Orchids

THE MARIE SELBY BOTANICAL GARDENS

If an organism doesn't reproduce, it won't survive. So the most important thing any organism can do is "make more of itself." When it comes to reproducing, few plants or animals are as clever as bucket orchids.

THE MARIE SELBY BOTANICAL GARDENS

Like other flowers, orchids need to be pollinated or **fertilized** before they can make seeds. They depend on insects to carry pollen from one flower to another, and orchids use special tricks to attract the pollen carriers. Some orchids provide nectar for insects to eat. Other orchids lure insects with delicious smells. But the bucket orchid has its own bag of tricks.

The bucket orchid is named for the bucket-shaped trap that takes up most of its flower. Its "bucket" is about the size of a toy teacup, and it's filled with fluid. Like many other orchids, the bucket orchid attracts bees with a sweet-smelling, waxy substance.

24

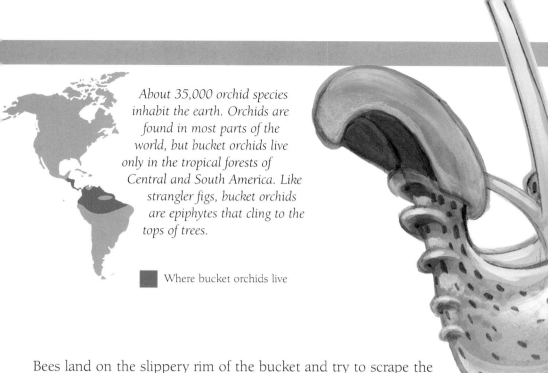

About 35,000 orchid species inhabit the earth. Orchids are found in most parts of the world, but bucket orchids live only in the tropical forests of Central and South America. Like strangler figs, bucket orchids are epiphytes that cling to the tops of trees.

■ Where bucket orchids live

Bees land on the slippery rim of the bucket and try to scrape the sweet substance onto their legs. Before long, though, one of the bees slips into the bucket and sinks to the bottom.

The orchid does not drown its victim. The flower has a little "step" inside that leads to an escape tunnel. When the bee climbs into the tunnel—surprise! The tunnel slams down, gluing two little packets of pollen to the bee's back. The orchid flower pins the bee down for several minutes—long enough to ensure that the pollen is firmly in place. Then it releases the waterlogged insect.

The orchid flower traps only the first bee that falls into its bucket. Other bees fall in, but they crawl through the escape tunnel without getting pinned inside. If the orchid is lucky, though, a bee carrying pollen from a *different* bucket orchid will pass through. When it does, the pollen on the bee's back is picked off by a little hook in the escape tunnel, and this pollen fertilizes the orchid. Then the bucket orchid "shuts its trap" and begins growing the seeds for a new generation of flowering tricksters.

PROTECTIVE PARENTS
Poison Arrow Frogs

Poison arrow frogs get their name from the highly toxic substances found in their skin. About 100 species of poison arrow frogs live the tropical rain forests of South and Central America—moist, humid places that provide homes for water-loving amphibians like frogs, toads, and salamanders.

Reproduction is essential to animals as well as plants. It's especially important to make sure that young animals survive to become adults. Baby animals face many dangers—they might get eaten, get lost, die of thirst, or even starve to death. These risks are enough to drive poison arrow frog mothers right up a tree.

ART WOLFE

Poison arrow frogs don't take chances with their young. Parents hide their small batch of two to twenty eggs under damp leaves and guard the eggs until they hatch. In some species, Mom then gives her newly-hatched tadpoles a "piggyback ride."

Where poison arrow frogs live

Carrying a tadpole on her back, the mother frog begins a long, hard climb up a nearby tree. She is searching for "swimming pools in the sky"—actually epiphytes called **tank bromeliads** (BRO-MIL-E-ADS). Bromeliads catch rain water in the base of their leaves. When the mother frog finds a bromeliad pool, she releases her tadpole into the water. She won't rest until she finds a watery home for each of her tadpoles.

Life is pretty good for a tadpole in its own swimming pool. It feeds on mosquito larvae and other insects that live in the water, but the tadpole has a big appetite, and sometimes the food runs out. Mom comes to the rescue. Every day, she climbs back up the tree and drops an unfertilized egg into each pool for the tadpoles to eat. By delivering "groceries," the mother frog gives her tadpoles the best possible chance of growing up and adding their voices to the rain forest chorus.

CHAMPIONS OF CHANGE
Human Beings

Sooner or later, one of nature's laws affects all living things: the law of change. Some organisms are good at adapting to change. Bacteria, for instance, constantly evolve into new forms that can survive in new ways or new places. However, among the world's larger animals, human beings are the "change champions."

LARRY MISHKAR

Human societies have coped with change for thousands of years. We have survived ice ages, droughts, volcanic eruptions, and countless other challenges. How have we done it? By using our special tools. One important tool is the human hand, which lets us pick up and move objects, plant crops, start warm fires, and build shelters. But an even more important tool is our **intelligence**.

Intelligence has given us the ability to figure out what's around us and how we can use our environment to survive. Our intelligence lets us respond to whatever happens, and even allows us to plan for what *will* happen in the future.

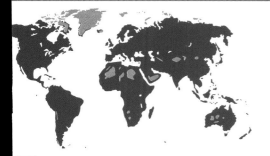

Where people *don't* live

People have colonized almost every habitat on our planet. We have learned to live in dry deserts, frigid polar regions, and steamy jungles.

LARRY MISHKAR

For millions of years, nature gave us changes we could handle with our intelligence. During cold times, people learned to wear clothes and find shelters so they could stay warm. During dry periods, people learned to store water or dig wells.

Over the last few thousand years, however, human activities have created even bigger changes. For example, by cutting down forests, we have raised the temperatures and lowered the amount of rainfall in some places. In other places, poor farming practices have caused soil to wash away, making it impossible to grow food on the land. Toxic chemicals made by people have poisoned streams, lakes, and oceans that once gave us healthy fish and clean water. All of these changes are more difficult to handle than the changes nature has thrown at us.

So far we've been able to use our intelligence in adapting to change. But as the human population gets larger and larger, our world is changing faster and faster. Will we survive? Probably. But what kind of world we live in depends on how well we plan for the future. If we hope to remain the champions of change, we'll have to use our smarts in new and better ways.

More About Smart Survivors

ERN MAINKA

There are thousands of "smart survivors" that we couldn't fit into this book. Scientists believe that between 10 and 30 *million* species of plants and animals live on our planet, and each species has its own ways of doing things. Scientists sometimes refer to the variety of different plants and animals on Earth as **biodiversity** (BIO-DI-VER-SI-TEE). The highest biodiversity probably exists in tropical rain forests and on coral reefs. Millions and millions of plants and animals make their homes in these places. But biodiversity is all around us. Hundreds of species of plants and animals—from birds to microscopic worms—live in our own back yards.

Yet each year, many species of plants and animals become extinct. People hunt some species to extinction, but most species disappear because people destroy their habitats.

The cutting and burning of rain forests, for example, has already destroyed thousands of species of insects and plants. Unless people stop this destruction, *millions* more may disappear.

Why is this a problem? First of all, each species of plant or animal is valuable just because it exists. Secondly, many of these plants and animals are useful to us. For instance, scientists have discovered a plant in Madagascar that helps control a disease called leukemia. Plants are also used to cure

DAVID HISER/PHOTOGRAPHERS/ASPEN